W9-AVM-268

APR 2019

my LITTLE PONY

Friendship is Magic
VOL. 16

WRITTEN BY **Heather Nuhfer**

ART BY **Amy Mebberson**

COLORS BY **Heather Breckel**

LETTERS BY **Neil Uyetake**

EDITED BY **Bobby Curnow**

ABDOBOOKS.COM

Reinforced library bound edition published in 2019 by Spotlight, a division of ABDO, PO Box 398166, Minneapolis, Minnesota 55439. Spotlight produces high-quality reinforced library bound editions for schools and libraries. Published by agreement with IDW.

Printed in the United States of America, North Mankato, Minnesota.
092018
012019

 THIS BOOK CONTAINS RECYCLED MATERIALS

Licensed By:

Library of Congress Control Number: 2018940477

Publisher's Cataloging-in-Publication Data

Names: Cook, Katie, author. Nuhfer, Heather, author. | Price, Andy; Breckel, Heather; Uyetake, Neil; Hickey, Brenda; Mebberson, Amy, illustrators.
Title: My little pony: friendship is magic / writers: Katie Cook; Heather Nuhfer; art: Andy Price; Heather Breckel; Neil Uyetake; Brenda Hickey; Amy Mebberson.
Description: Minneapolis, MN : Spotlight, 2019 | Series: My little pony: friendship is magic set 2
Summary: Welcome to Ponyville, home of Twilight Sparkle, Rainbow Dash, Rarity, Fluttershy, Pinkie Pie, Applejack, and all your other favorite ponies! When evil forces threaten the ponies' good life, it's up to the Mane Six to use the Magic of Friendship to face new challenges and conquer their fears.
Identifiers: ISBN 9781532142253 (v. 9; lib. bdg.) | ISBN 9781532142260 (v. 10; lib. bdg.) | ISBN 9781532142277 (v. 11; lib. bdg.) | ISBN 9781532142284 (v. 12; lib. bdg.) | ISBN 9781532142291 (v. 13; lib. bdg.) | ISBN 9781532142307 (v. 14; lib. bdg.) | ISBN 9781532142314 (v. 15; lib. bdg.) | ISBN 9781532142321 (v. 16; lib. bdg.)
Subjects: LCSH: My Little Pony (Trademark)--Juvenile fiction. | Hardware stores--Juvenile fiction. | Ponies--Juvenile fiction. | Fireworks--Juvenile fiction. | Dating--Juvenile fiction. | Love--Juvenile fiction. | Kings, queens, rulers, etc.--Juvenile fiction | Pirates--Juvenile fiction. | Book-worms--Juvenile fiction. | Libraries--Juvenile fiction. | Comic books, strips, etc.--Juvenile fiction.
Classification: DDC 741.5--dc23

Spotlight

A Division of ABDO
abdobooks.com

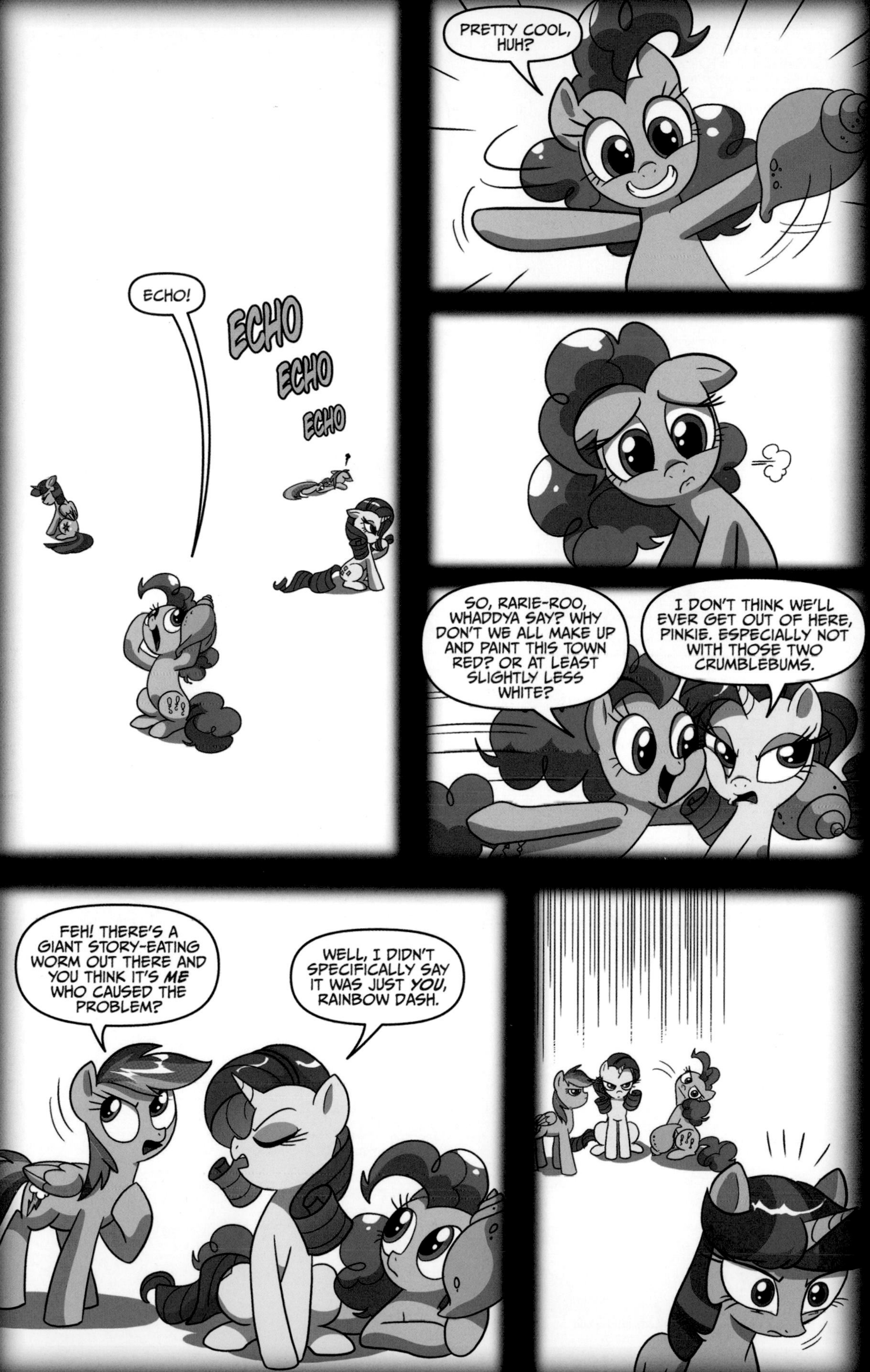
ECHO!
ECHO
ECHO
ECHO
PRETTY COOL, HUH?
SO, RARIE-ROO, WHADDYA SAY? WHY DON'T WE ALL MAKE UP AND PAINT THIS TOWN RED? OR AT LEAST SLIGHTLY LESS WHITE?
I DON'T THINK WE'LL EVER GET OUT OF HERE, PINKIE. ESPECIALLY NOT WITH THOSE TWO CRUMBLEBUMS.
FEH! THERE'S A GIANT STORY-EATING WORM OUT THERE AND YOU THINK IT'S *ME* WHO CAUSED THE PROBLEM?
WELL, I DIDN'T SPECIFICALLY SAY IT WAS JUST *YOU*, RAINBOW DASH.

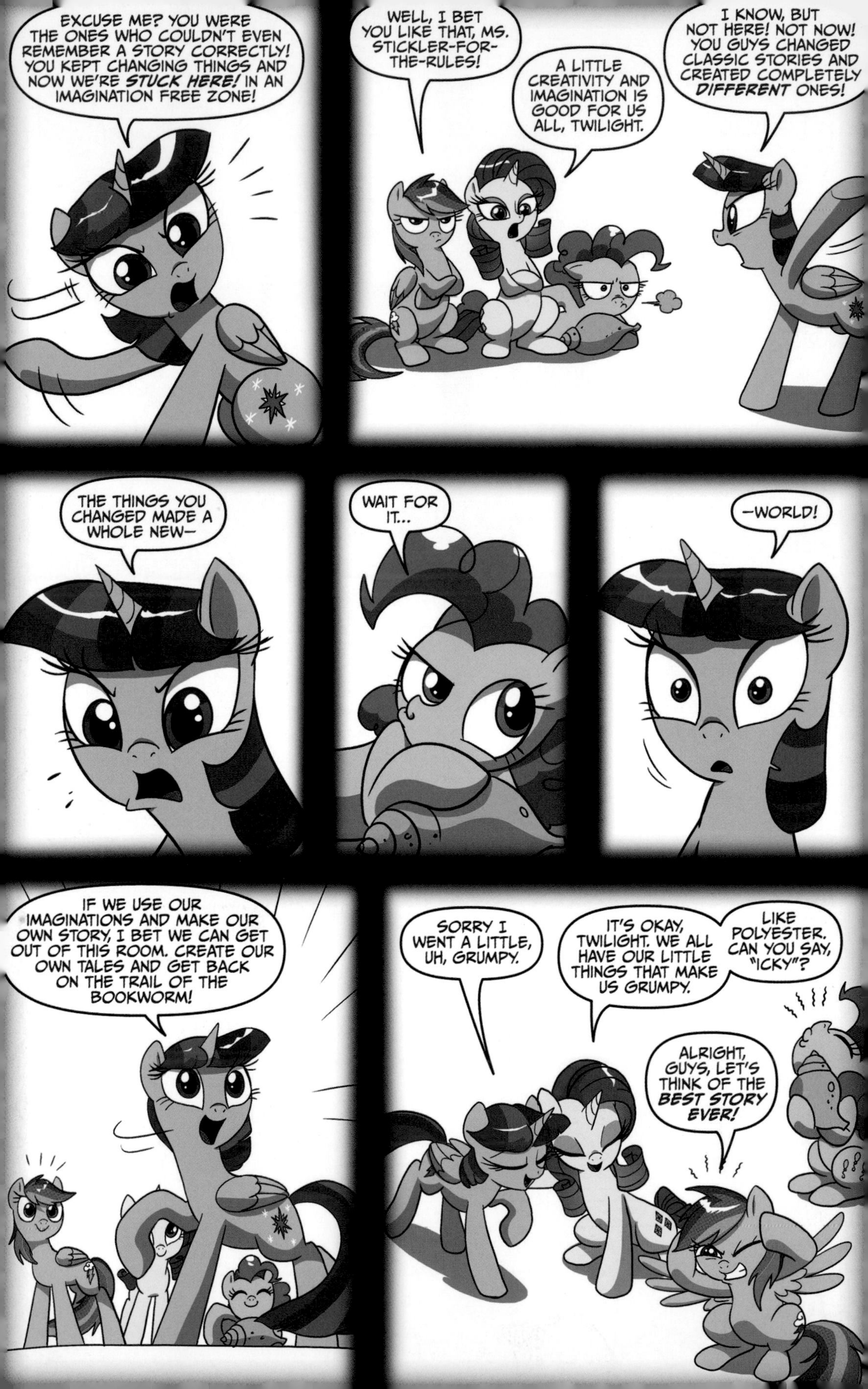
EXCUSE ME? YOU WERE THE ONES WHO COULDN'T EVEN REMEMBER A STORY CORRECTLY! YOU KEPT CHANGING THINGS AND NOW WE'RE *STUCK HERE!* IN AN IMAGINATION FREE ZONE!
WELL, I BET YOU LIKE THAT, MS. STICKLER-FOR-THE-RULES!
A LITTLE CREATIVITY AND IMAGINATION IS GOOD FOR US ALL, TWILIGHT.
I KNOW, BUT NOT HERE! NOT NOW! YOU GUYS CHANGED CLASSIC STORIES AND CREATED COMPLETELY *DIFFERENT* ONES!
THE THINGS YOU CHANGED MADE A WHOLE NEW–
WAIT FOR IT...
–WORLD!
IF WE USE OUR IMAGINATIONS AND MAKE OUR OWN STORY, I BET WE CAN GET OUT OF THIS ROOM. CREATE OUR OWN TALES AND GET BACK ON THE TRAIL OF THE BOOKWORM!
SORRY I WENT A LITTLE, UH, GRUMPY.
IT'S OKAY, TWILIGHT. WE ALL HAVE OUR LITTLE THINGS THAT MAKE US GRUMPY.
LIKE POLYESTER. CAN YOU SAY, "ICKY"?
ALRIGHT, GUYS, LET'S THINK OF THE *BEST STORY EVER!*

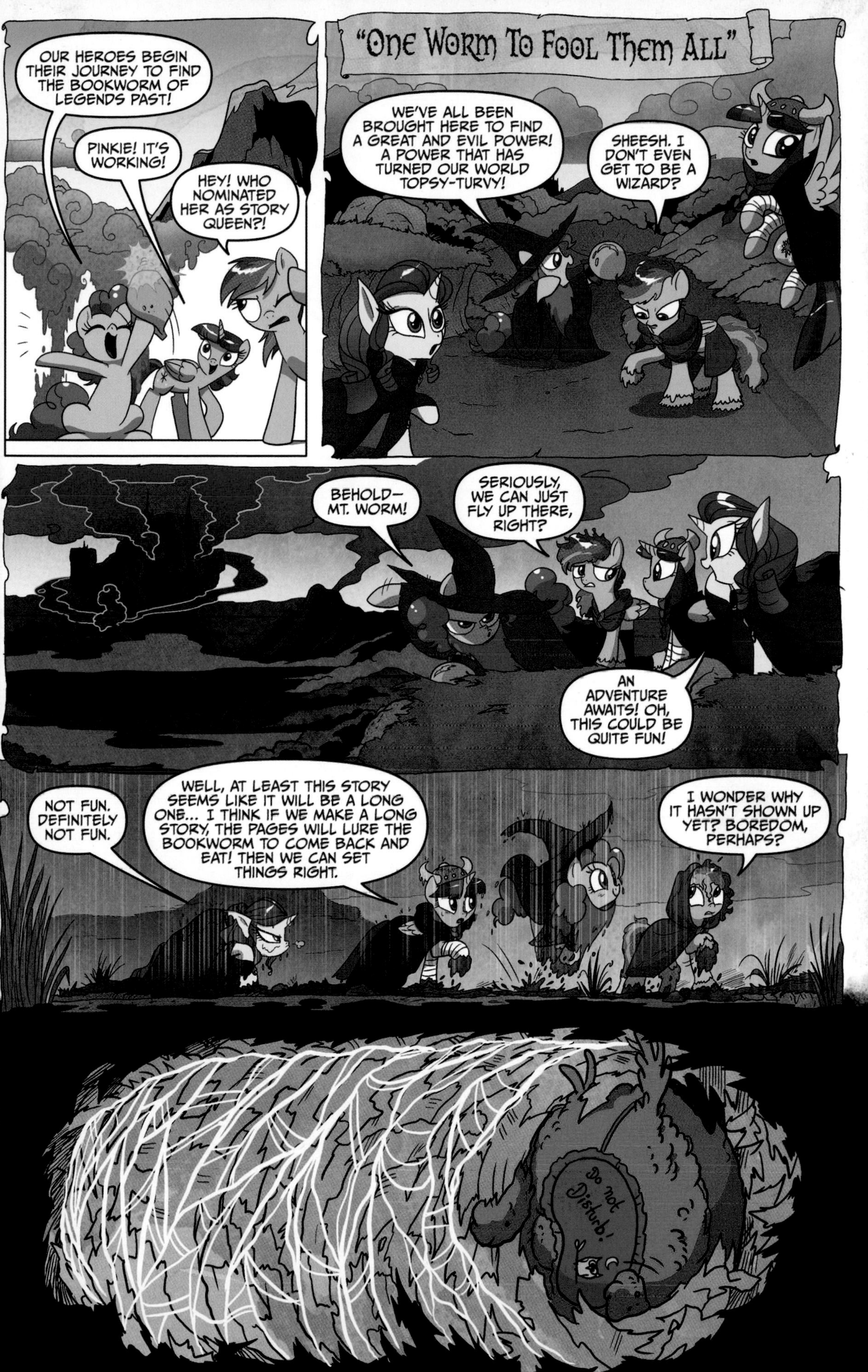
OUR HEROES BEGIN THEIR JOURNEY TO FIND THE BOOKWORM OF LEGENDS PAST!
PINKIE! IT'S WORKING!
HEY! WHO NOMINATED HER AS STORY QUEEN?!
"ONE WORM TO FOOL THEM ALL"
WE'VE ALL BEEN BROUGHT HERE TO FIND A GREAT AND EVIL POWER! A POWER THAT HAS TURNED OUR WORLD TOPSY-TURVY!
SHEESH. I DON'T EVEN GET TO BE A WIZARD?
BEHOLD— MT. WORM!
SERIOUSLY, WE CAN JUST FLY UP THERE, RIGHT?
AN ADVENTURE AWAITS! OH, THIS COULD BE QUITE FUN!
NOT FUN. DEFINITELY NOT FUN.
WELL, AT LEAST THIS STORY SEEMS LIKE IT WILL BE A LONG ONE... I THINK IF WE MAKE A LONG STORY, THE PAGES WILL LURE THE BOOKWORM TO COME BACK AND EAT! THEN WE CAN SET THINGS RIGHT.
I WONDER WHY IT HASN'T SHOWN UP YET? BOREDOM, PERHAPS?
Do not Disturb!

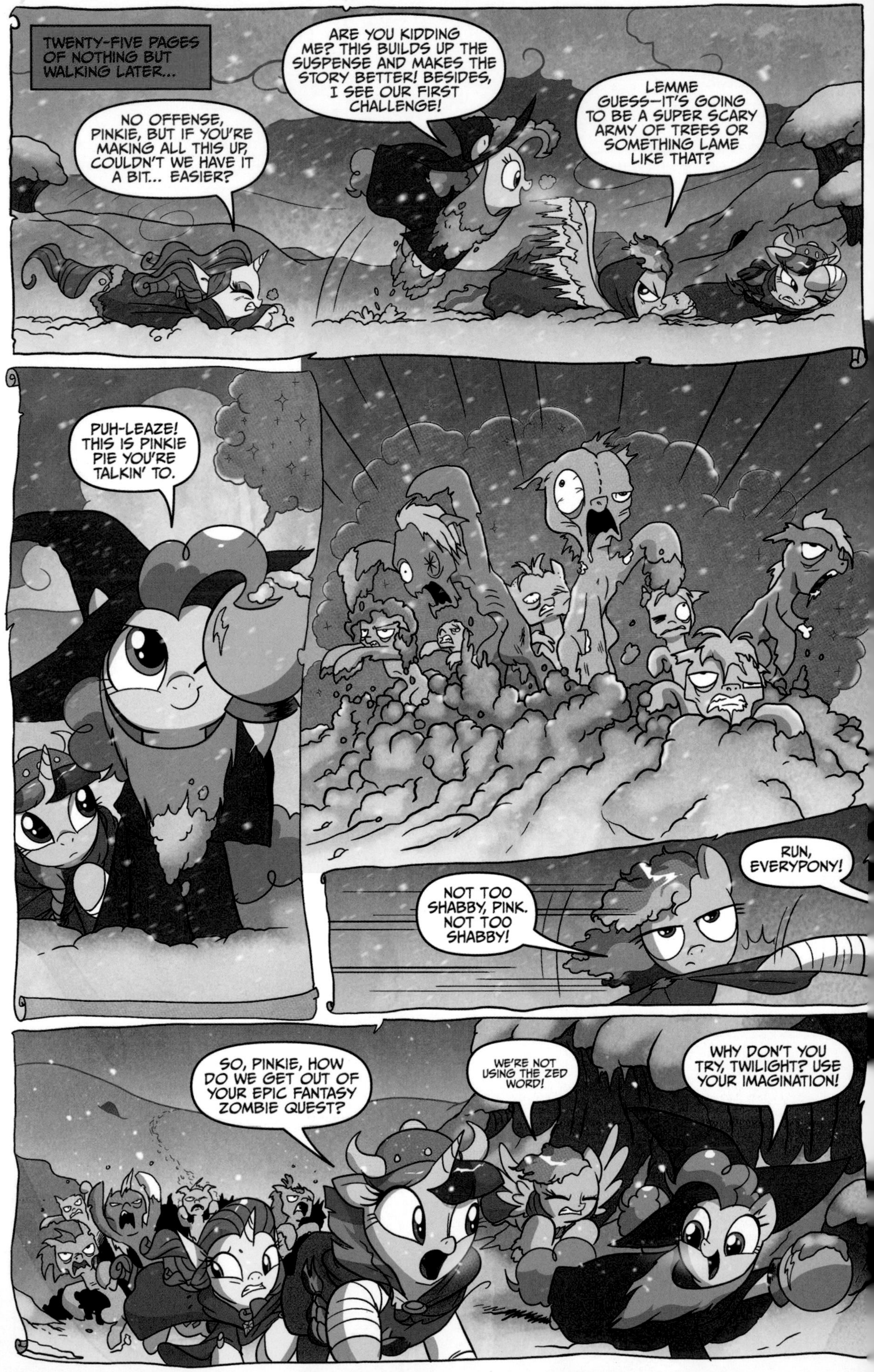
TWENTY-FIVE PAGES OF NOTHING BUT WALKING LATER...
NO OFFENSE, PINKIE, BUT IF YOU'RE MAKING ALL THIS UP, COULDN'T WE HAVE IT A BIT... EASIER?
ARE YOU KIDDING ME? THIS BUILDS UP THE SUSPENSE AND MAKES THE STORY BETTER! BESIDES, I SEE OUR FIRST CHALLENGE!
LEMME GUESS—IT'S GOING TO BE A SUPER SCARY ARMY OF TREES OR SOMETHING LAME LIKE THAT?
PUH-LEAZE! THIS IS PINKIE PIE YOU'RE TALKIN' TO.
NOT TOO SHABBY, PINK. NOT TOO SHABBY!
RUN, EVERYPONY!
SO, PINKIE, HOW DO WE GET OUT OF YOUR EPIC FANTASY ZOMBIE QUEST?
WE'RE NOT USING THE ZED WORD!
WHY DON'T YOU TRY, TWILIGHT? USE YOUR IMAGINATION!

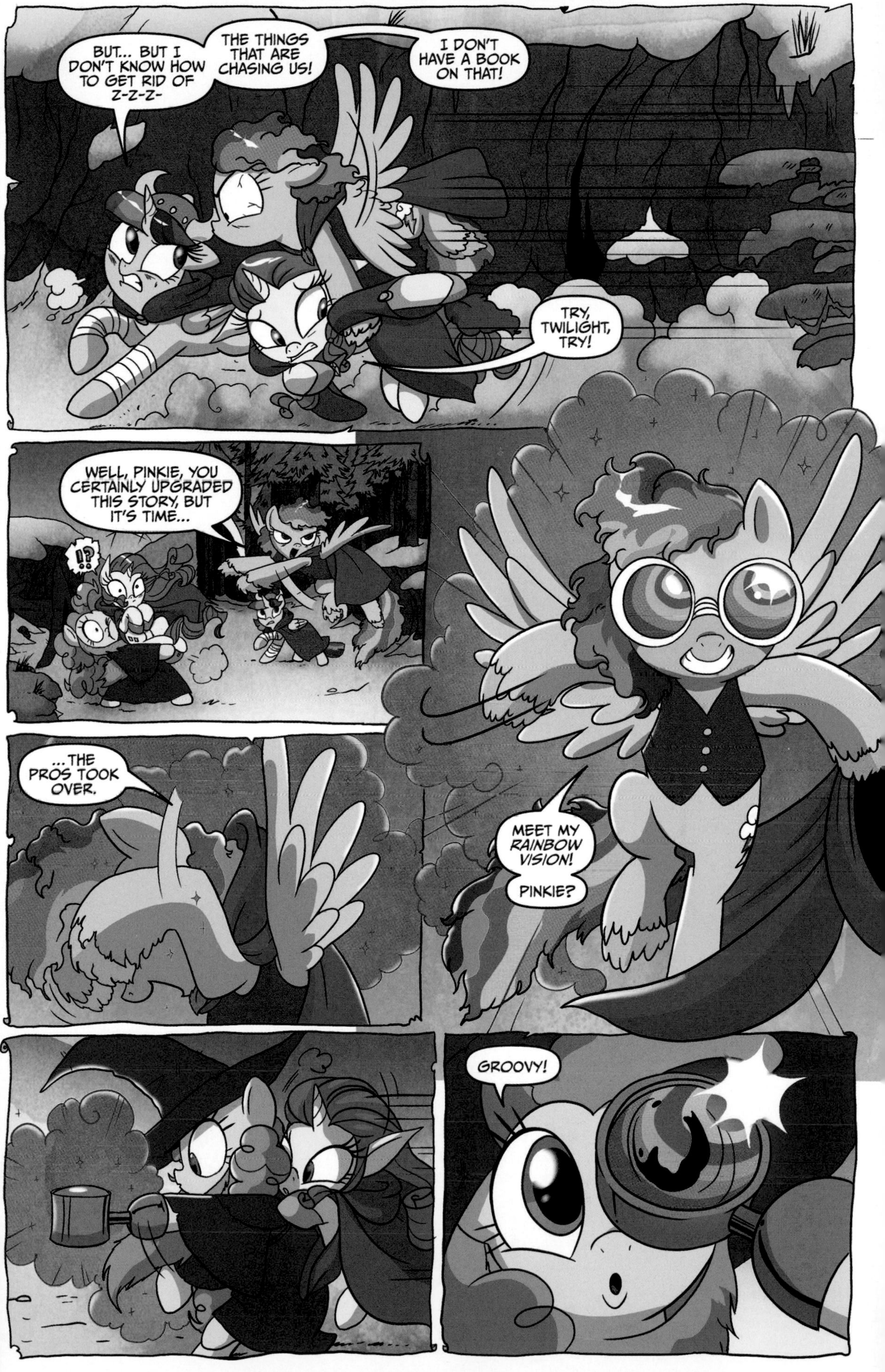
BUT... BUT I DON'T KNOW HOW TO GET RID OF Z-Z-Z-
THE THINGS THAT ARE CHASING US!
I DON'T HAVE A BOOK ON THAT!
TRY, TWILIGHT, TRY!
WELL, PINKIE, YOU CERTAINLY UPGRADED THIS STORY, BUT IT'S TIME...
!?
...THE PROS TOOK OVER.
MEET MY RAINBOW VISION!
PINKIE?
GROOVY!

BE FREE, MY ZED HEAD FRIENDS!

THANK YOU, MYSTERIOUS HERO!

ALL IN A DAY'S WORK, MISS. MY RAINBOWETTES AND I WILL ALWAYS BE HERE TO SAVE YOU.

OUR RIDE IS HERE!

HAVE A DASHING DAY.

"RAINBOWETTES?"

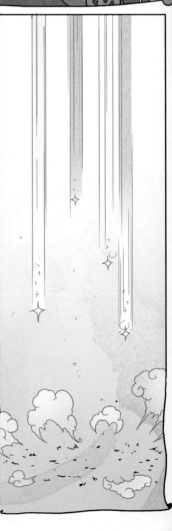

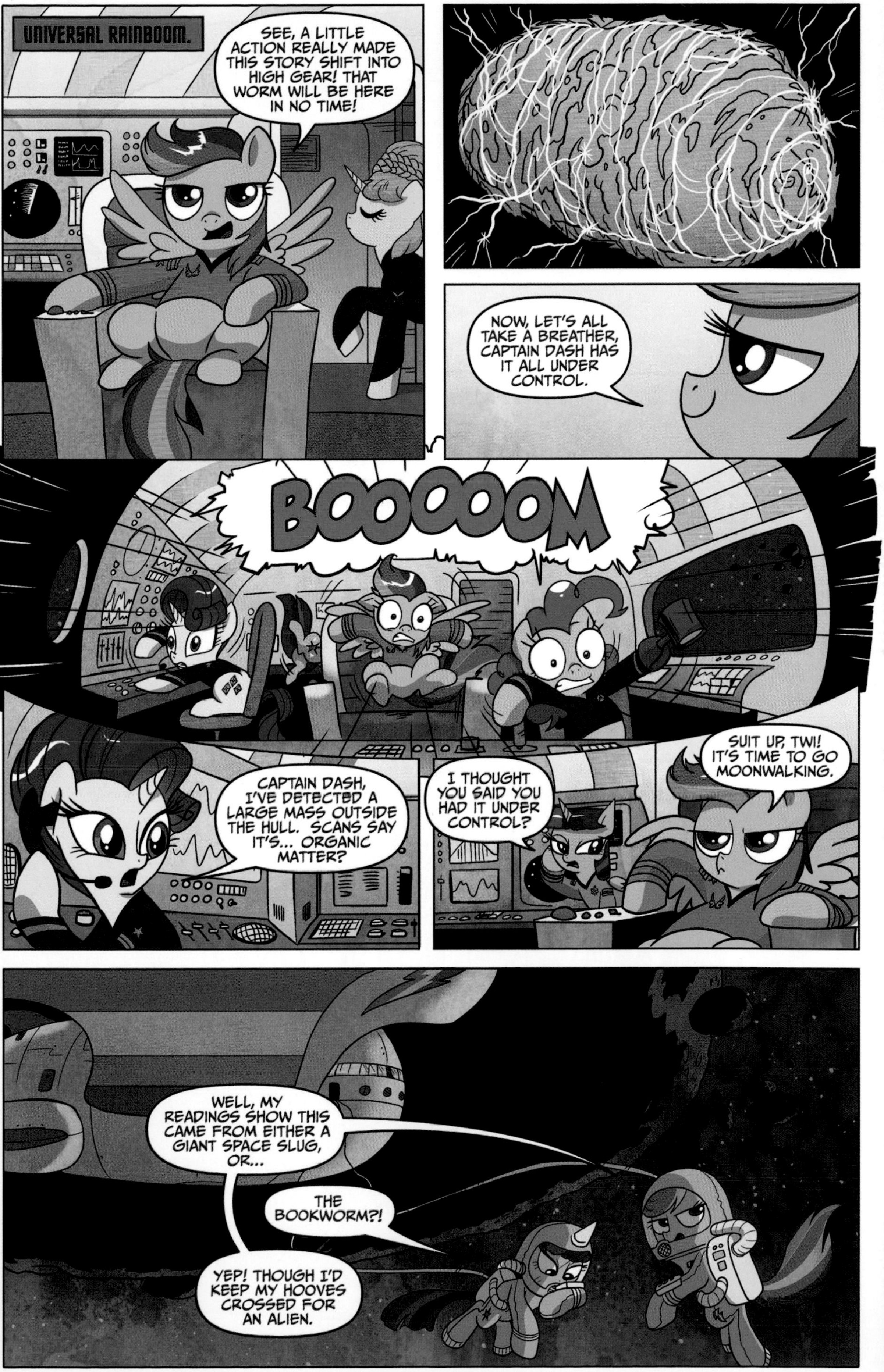
UNIVERSAL RAINBOOM.
SEE, A LITTLE ACTION REALLY MADE THIS STORY SHIFT INTO HIGH GEAR! THAT WORM WILL BE HERE IN NO TIME!
NOW, LET'S ALL TAKE A BREATHER, CAPTAIN DASH HAS IT ALL UNDER CONTROL.
BOOOOOM
CAPTAIN DASH, I'VE DETECTED A LARGE MASS OUTSIDE THE HULL. SCANS SAY IT'S... ORGANIC MATTER?
I THOUGHT YOU SAID YOU HAD IT UNDER CONTROL?
SUIT UP, TWI! IT'S TIME TO GO MOONWALKING.
WELL, MY READINGS SHOW THIS CAME FROM EITHER A GIANT SPACE SLUG, OR...
THE BOOKWORM?!
YEP! THOUGH I'D KEEP MY HOOVES CROSSED FOR AN ALIEN.

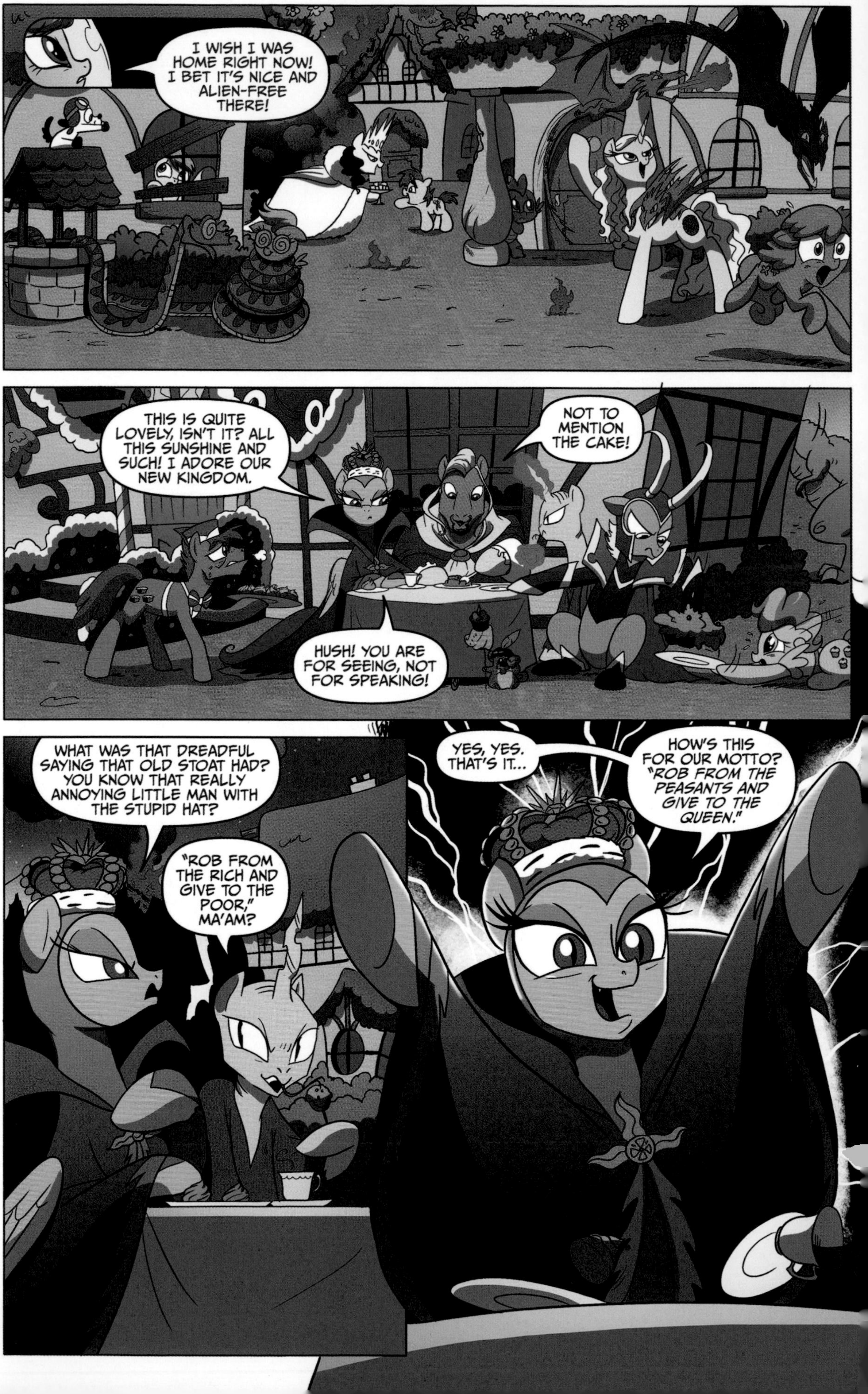
I WISH I WAS HOME RIGHT NOW! I BET IT'S NICE AND ALIEN-FREE THERE!
THIS IS QUITE LOVELY, ISN'T IT? ALL THIS SUNSHINE AND SUCH! I ADORE OUR NEW KINGDOM.
NOT TO MENTION THE CAKE!
HUSH! YOU ARE FOR SEEING, NOT FOR SPEAKING!
WHAT WAS THAT DREADFUL SAYING THAT OLD STOAT HAD? YOU KNOW THAT REALLY ANNOYING LITTLE MAN WITH THE STUPID HAT?
"ROB FROM THE RICH AND GIVE TO THE POOR," MA'AM?
YES, YES. THAT'S IT...
HOW'S THIS FOR OUR MOTTO? "ROB FROM THE PEASANTS AND GIVE TO THE QUEEN."

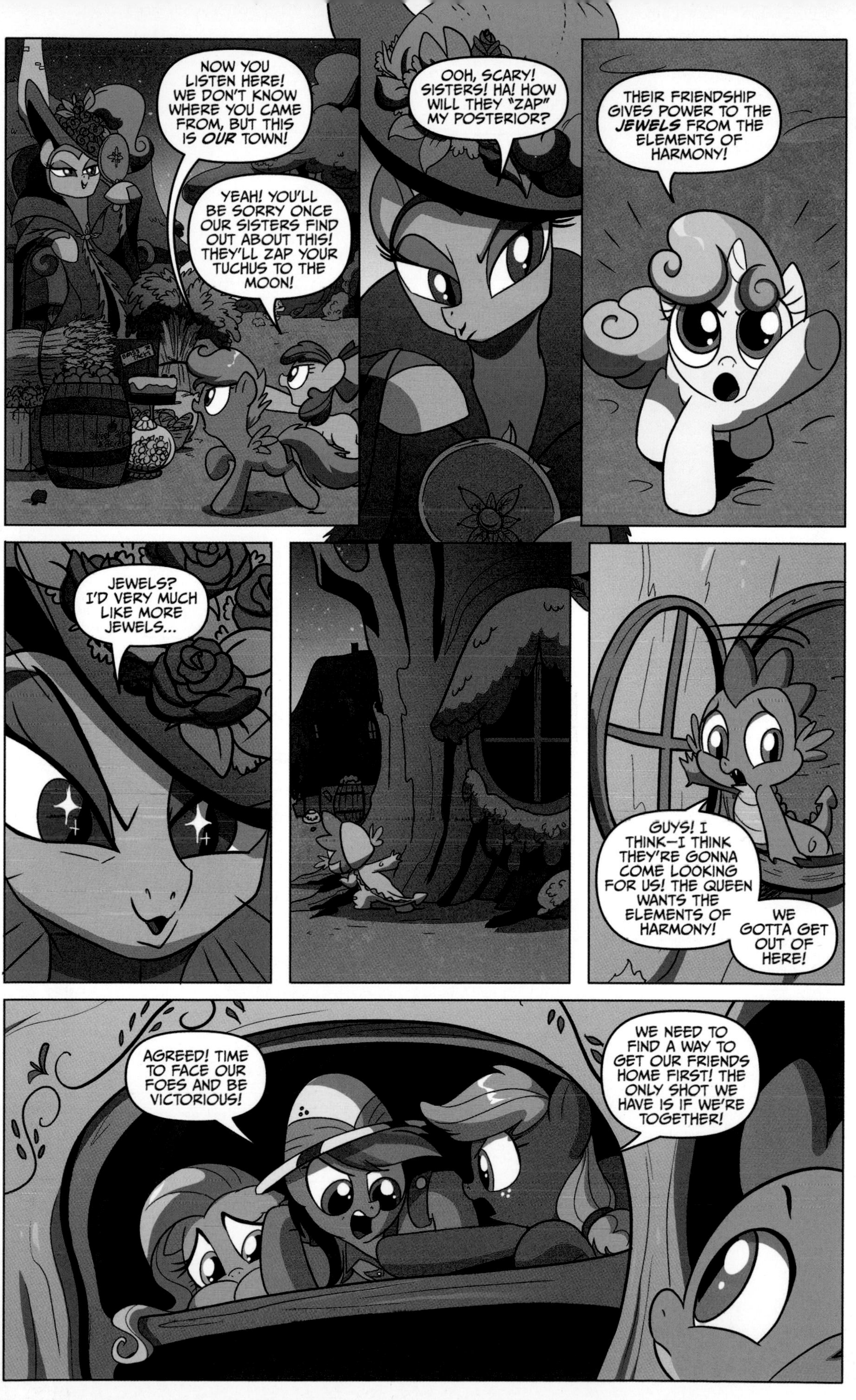
NOW YOU LISTEN HERE! WE DON'T KNOW WHERE YOU CAME FROM, BUT THIS IS *OUR* TOWN!
YEAH! YOU'LL BE SORRY ONCE OUR SISTERS FIND OUT ABOUT THIS! THEY'LL ZAP YOUR TUCHUS TO THE MOON!
OOH, SCARY! SISTERS! HA! HOW WILL THEY "ZAP" MY POSTERIOR?
THEIR FRIENDSHIP GIVES POWER TO THE ***JEWELS*** FROM THE ELEMENTS OF HARMONY!
JEWELS? I'D VERY MUCH LIKE MORE JEWELS...
GUYS! I THINK—I THINK THEY'RE GONNA COME LOOKING FOR US! THE QUEEN WANTS THE ELEMENTS OF HARMONY!
WE GOTTA GET OUT OF HERE!
AGREED! TIME TO FACE OUR FOES AND BE VICTORIOUS!
WE NEED TO FIND A WAY TO GET OUR FRIENDS HOME FIRST! THE ONLY SHOT WE HAVE IS IF WE'RE TOGETHER!

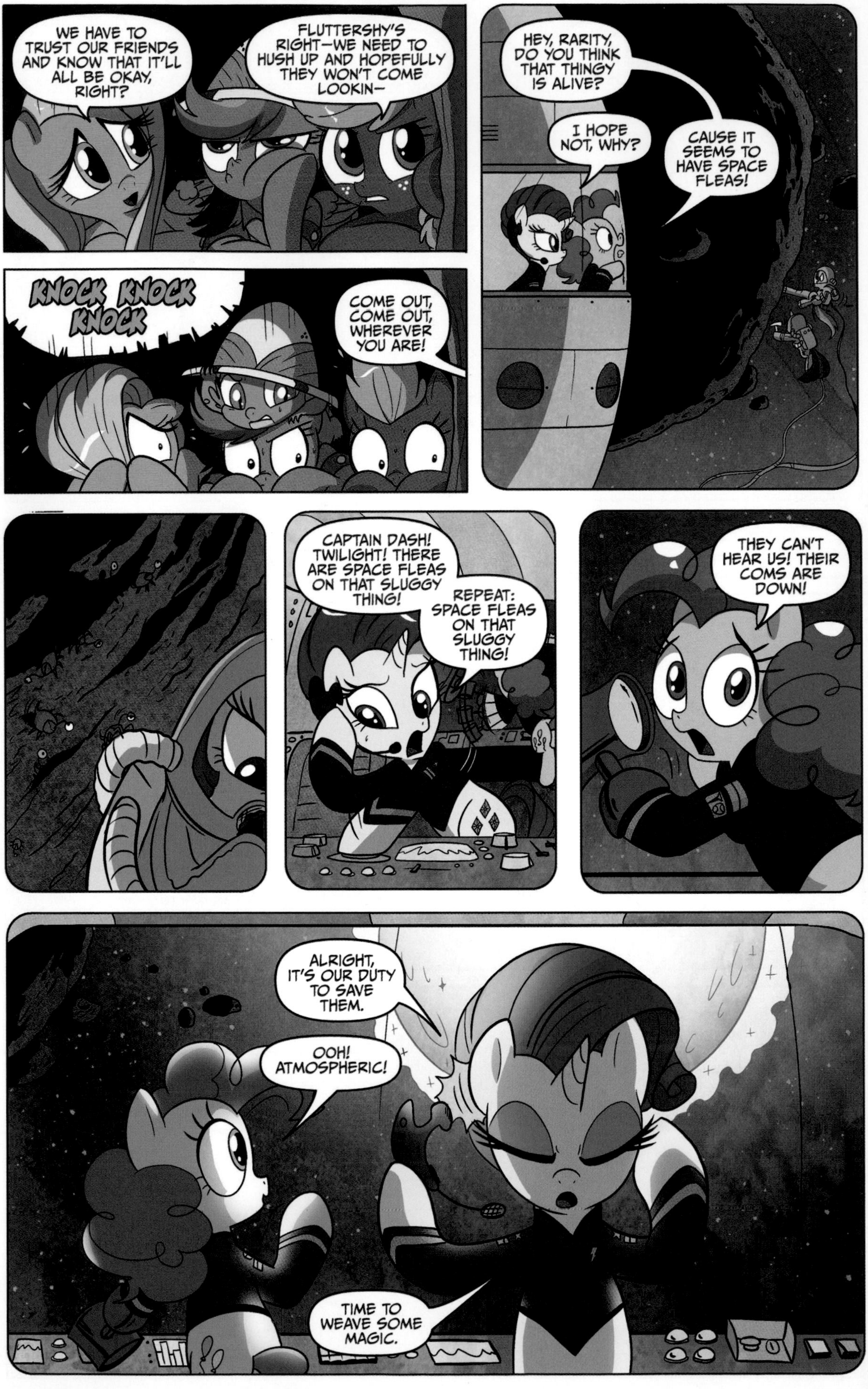
WE HAVE TO TRUST OUR FRIENDS AND KNOW THAT IT'LL ALL BE OKAY, RIGHT?
FLUTTERSHY'S RIGHT—WE NEED TO HUSH UP AND HOPEFULLY THEY WON'T COME LOOKIN—
KNOCK KNOCK KNOCK
COME OUT, COME OUT, WHEREVER YOU ARE!
HEY, RARITY, DO YOU THINK THAT THINGY IS ALIVE?
I HOPE NOT, WHY?
CAUSE IT SEEMS TO HAVE SPACE FLEAS!
CAPTAIN DASH! TWILIGHT! THERE ARE SPACE FLEAS ON THAT SLUGGY THING!
REPEAT: SPACE FLEAS ON THAT SLUGGY THING!
THEY CAN'T HEAR US! THEIR COMS ARE DOWN!
ALRIGHT, IT'S OUR DUTY TO SAVE THEM.
OOH! ATMOSPHERIC!
TIME TO WEAVE SOME MAGIC.

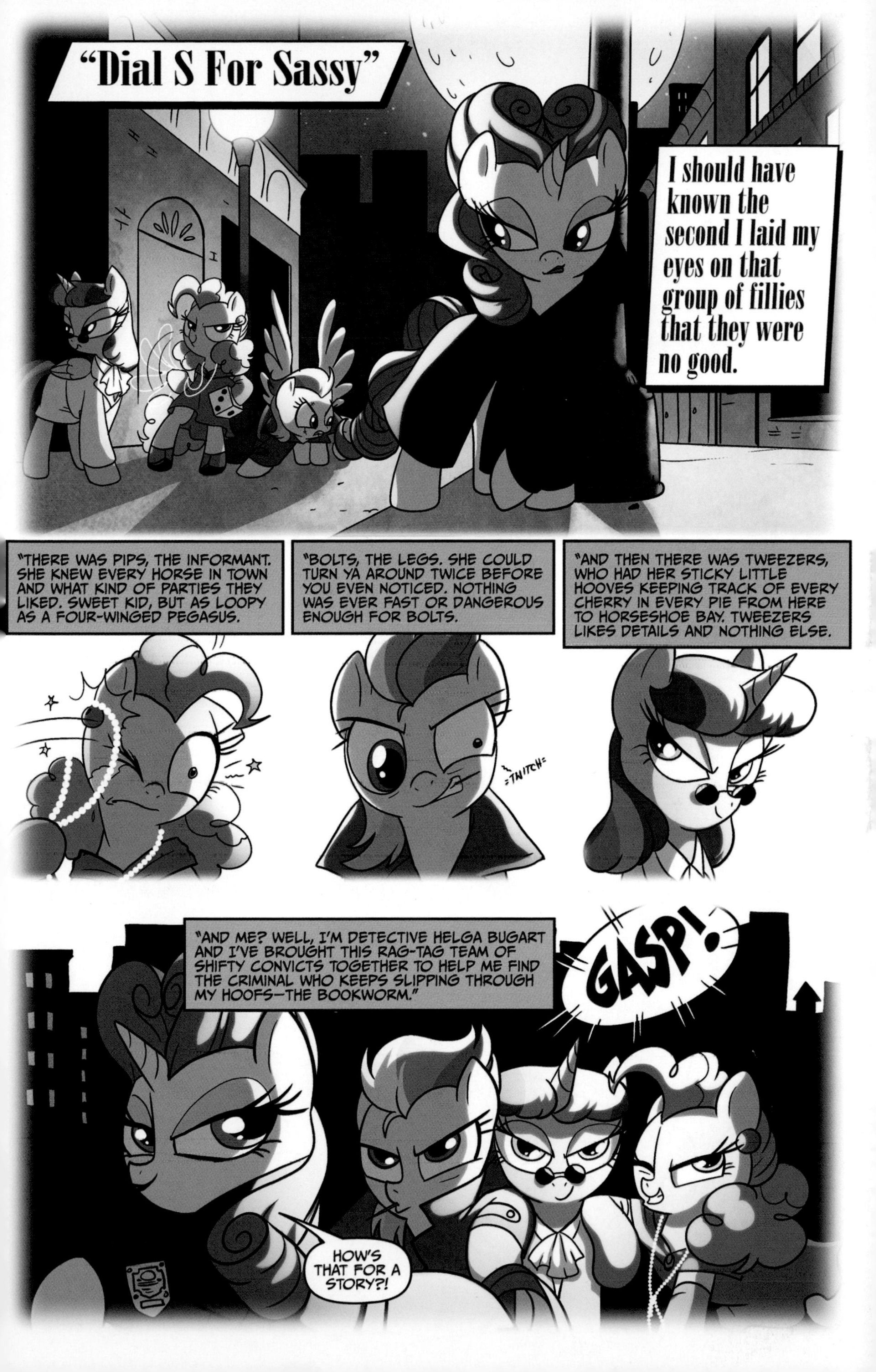
"Dial S For Sassy"
I should have known the second I laid my eyes on that group of fillies that they were no good.
"THERE WAS PIPS, THE INFORMANT. SHE KNEW EVERY HORSE IN TOWN AND WHAT KIND OF PARTIES THEY LIKED. SWEET KID, BUT AS LOOPY AS A FOUR-WINGED PEGASUS.
"BOLTS, THE LEGS. SHE COULD TURN YA AROUND TWICE BEFORE YOU EVEN NOTICED. NOTHING WAS EVER FAST OR DANGEROUS ENOUGH FOR BOLTS.
"AND THEN THERE WAS TWEEZERS, WHO HAD HER STICKY LITTLE HOOVES KEEPING TRACK OF EVERY CHERRY IN EVERY PIE FROM HERE TO HORSESHOE BAY. TWEEZERS LIKES DETAILS AND NOTHING ELSE.
=TWITCH=
"AND ME? WELL, I'M DETECTIVE HELGA BUGART AND I'VE BROUGHT THIS RAG-TAG TEAM OF SHIFTY CONVICTS TOGETHER TO HELP ME FIND THE CRIMINAL WHO KEEPS SLIPPING THROUGH MY HOOFS—THE BOOKWORM."
GASP!
HOW'S THAT FOR A STORY?!

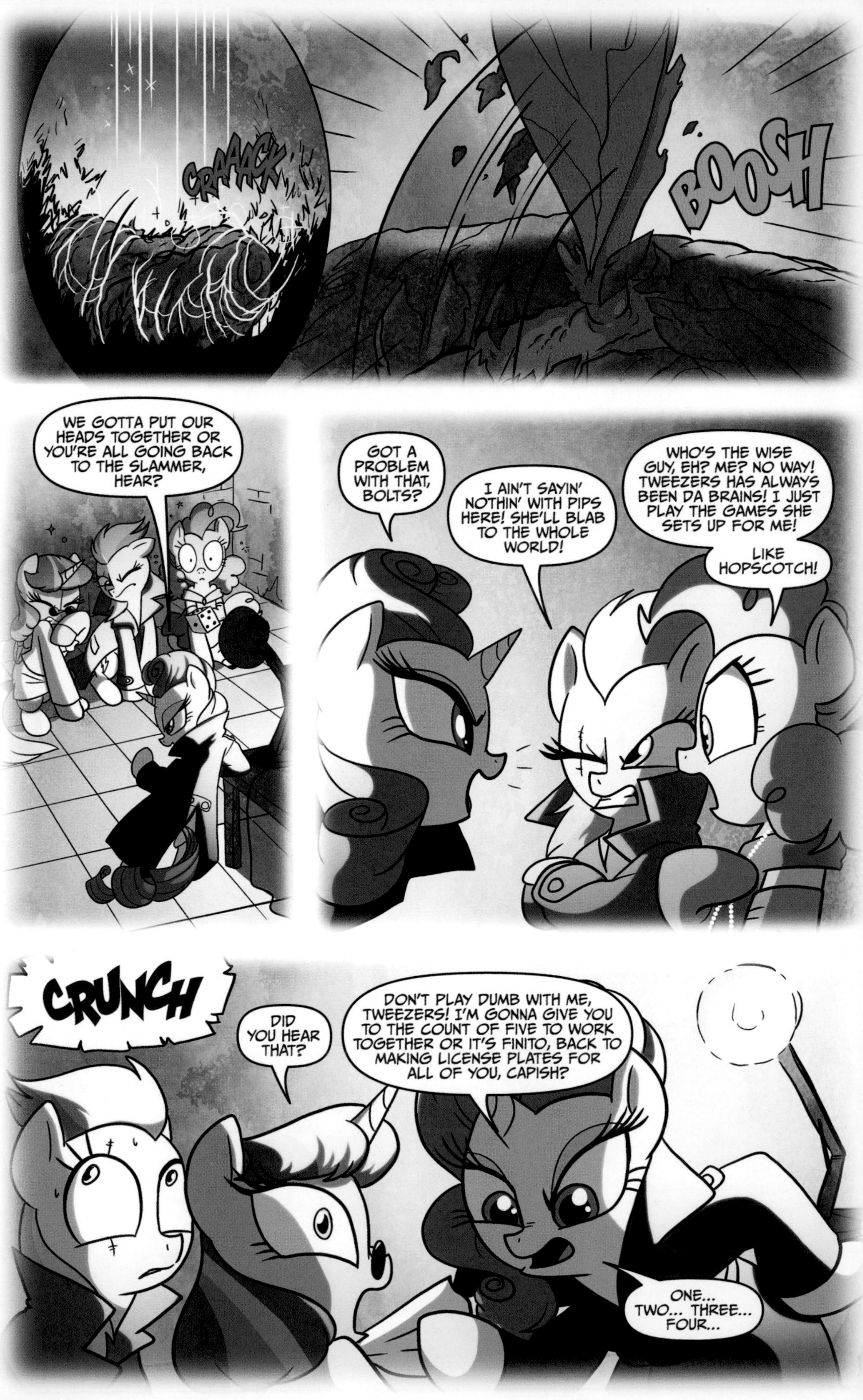
CRAAACK
BOOSH
WE GOTTA PUT OUR HEADS TOGETHER OR YOU'RE ALL GOING BACK TO THE SLAMMER, HEAR?
GOT A PROBLEM WITH THAT, BOLTS?
I AIN'T SAYIN' NOTHIN' WITH PIPS HERE! SHE'LL BLAB TO THE WHOLE WORLD!
WHO'S THE WISE GUY, EH? ME? NO WAY! TWEEZERS HAS ALWAYS BEEN DA BRAINS! I JUST PLAY THE GAMES SHE SETS UP FOR ME!
LIKE HOPSCOTCH!
CRUNCH
DID YOU HEAR THAT?
DON'T PLAY DUMB WITH ME, TWEEZERS! I'M GONNA GIVE YOU TO THE COUNT OF FIVE TO WORK TOGETHER OR IT'S FINITO, BACK TO MAKING LICENSE PLATES FOR ALL OF YOU, CAPISH?
ONE... TWO... THREE... FOUR...

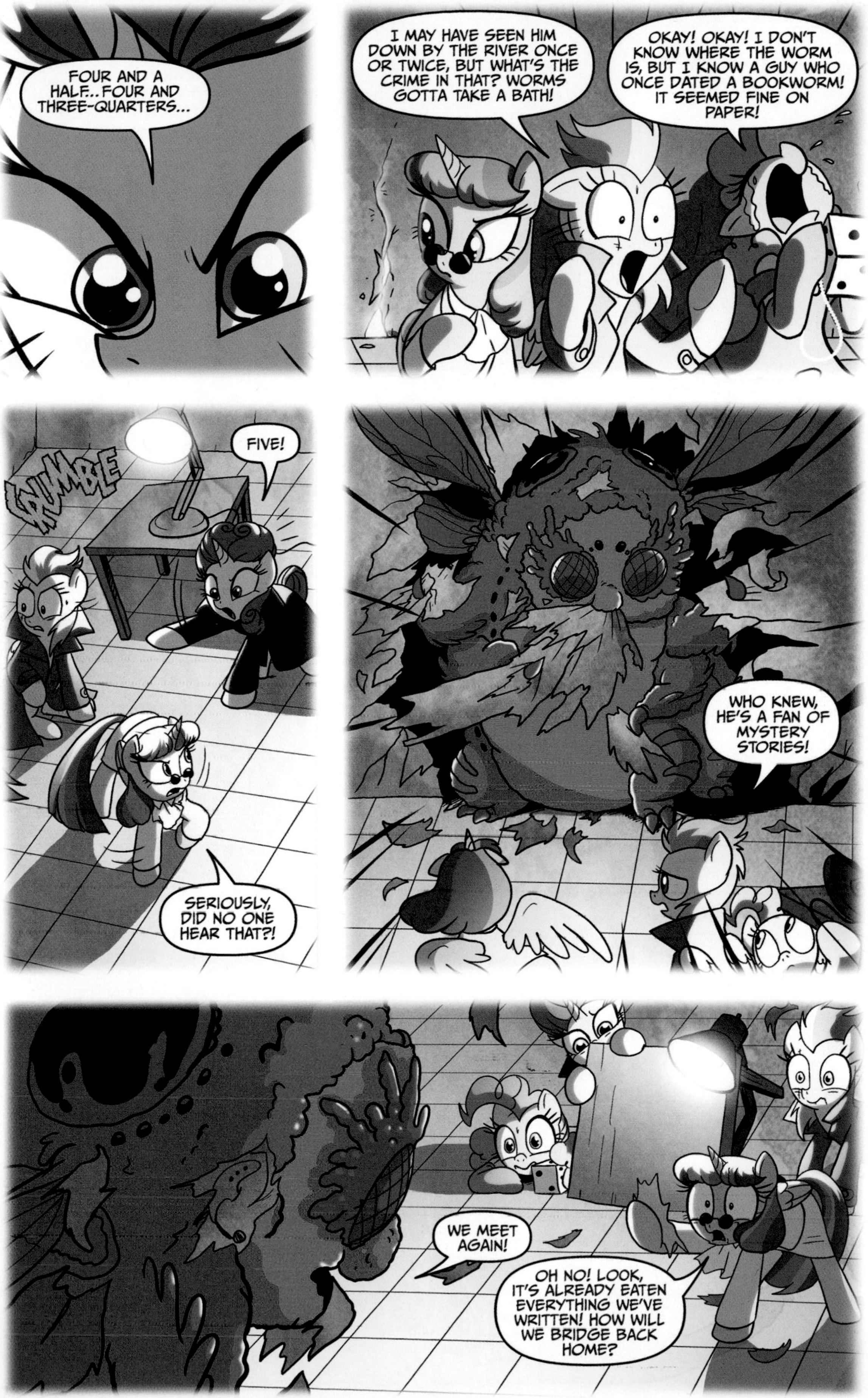

FOUR AND A HALF.. FOUR AND THREE-QUARTERS...
I MAY HAVE SEEN HIM DOWN BY THE RIVER ONCE OR TWICE, BUT WHAT'S THE CRIME IN THAT? WORMS GOTTA TAKE A BATH!
OKAY! OKAY! I DON'T KNOW WHERE THE WORM IS, BUT I KNOW A GUY WHO ONCE DATED A BOOKWORM! IT SEEMED FINE ON PAPER!
CRUMBLE
FIVE!
SERIOUSLY, DID NO ONE HEAR THAT?!
WHO KNEW, HE'S A FAN OF MYSTERY STORIES!
WE MEET AGAIN!
OH NO! LOOK, IT'S ALREADY EATEN EVERYTHING WE'VE WRITTEN! HOW WILL WE BRIDGE BACK HOME?

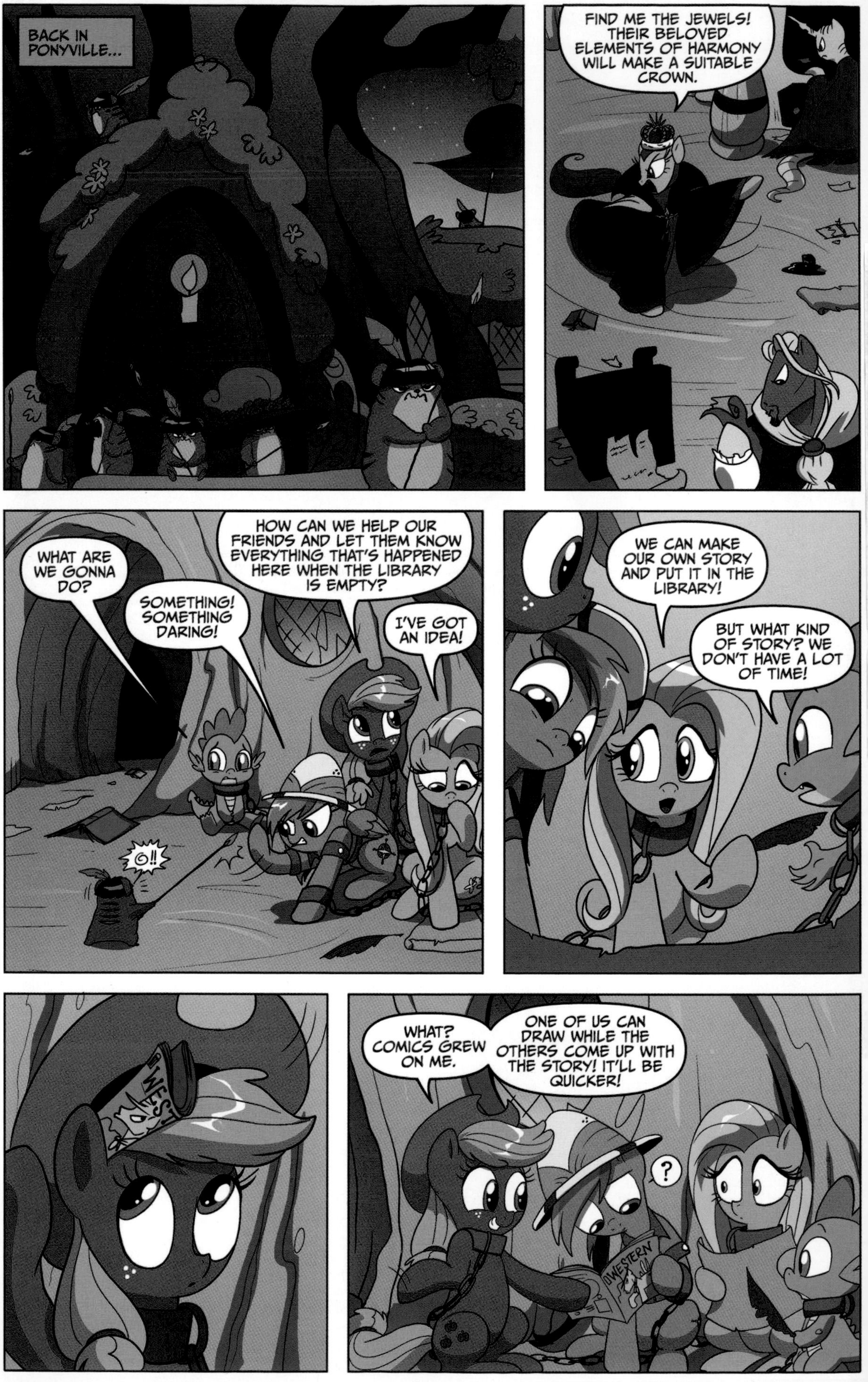
BACK IN PONYVILLE...
FIND ME THE JEWELS! THEIR BELOVED ELEMENTS OF HARMONY WILL MAKE A SUITABLE CROWN.
WHAT ARE WE GONNA DO?
SOMETHING! SOMETHING DARING!
HOW CAN WE HELP OUR FRIENDS AND LET THEM KNOW EVERYTHING THAT'S HAPPENED HERE WHEN THE LIBRARY IS EMPTY?
I'VE GOT AN IDEA!
G!!
WE CAN MAKE OUR OWN STORY AND PUT IT IN THE LIBRARY!
BUT WHAT KIND OF STORY? WE DON'T HAVE A LOT OF TIME!
WHAT? COMICS GREW ON ME.
ONE OF US CAN DRAW WHILE THE OTHERS COME UP WITH THE STORY! IT'LL BE QUICKER!
?
WESTERN

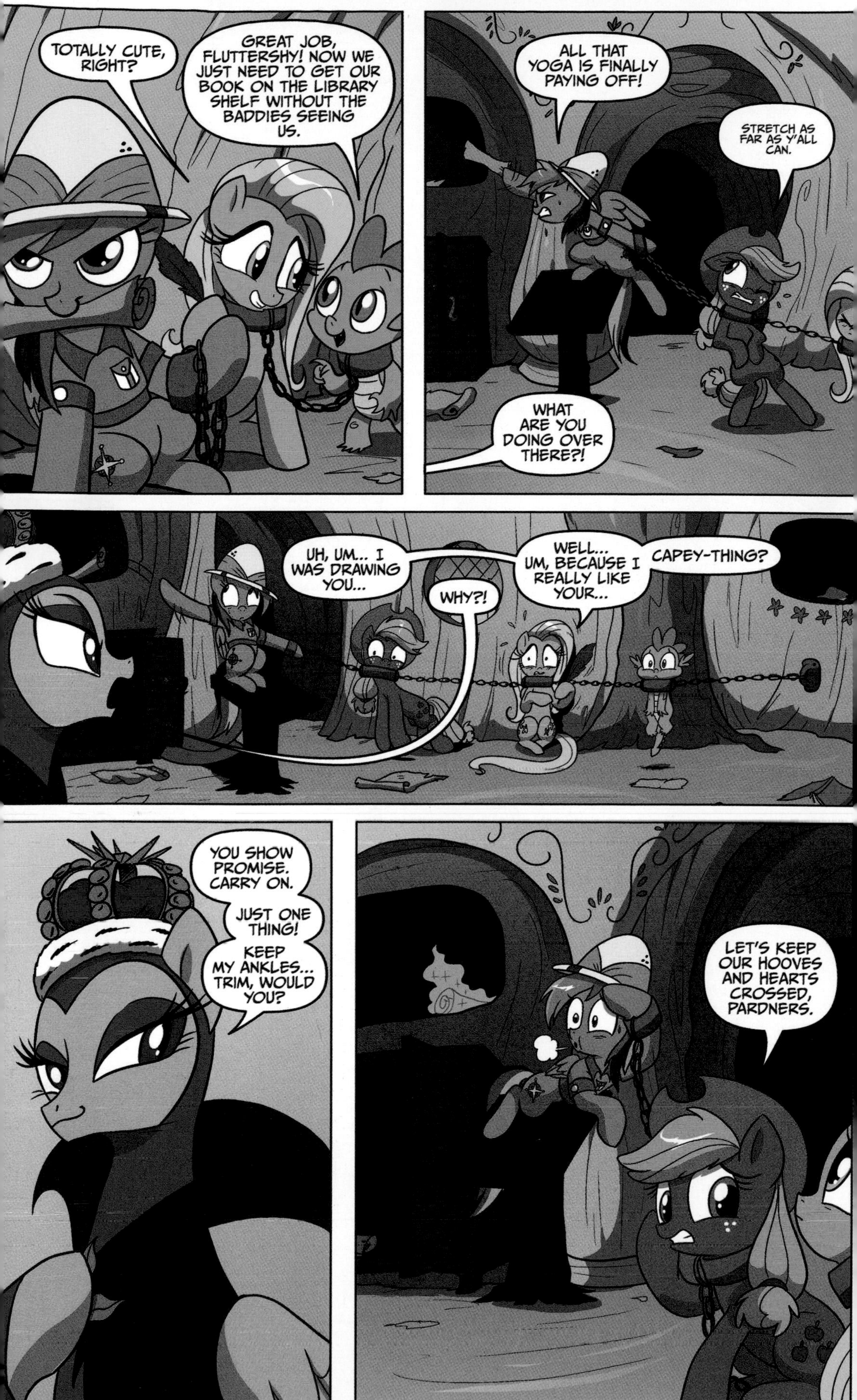

TOTALLY CUTE, RIGHT?
GREAT JOB, FLUTTERSHY! NOW WE JUST NEED TO GET OUR BOOK ON THE LIBRARY SHELF WITHOUT THE BADDIES SEEING US.
ALL THAT YOGA IS FINALLY PAYING OFF!
STRETCH AS FAR AS Y'ALL CAN.
WHAT ARE YOU DOING OVER THERE?!
UH, UM... I WAS DRAWING YOU...
WHY?!
WELL... UM, BECAUSE I REALLY LIKE YOUR...
CAPEY-THING?
YOU SHOW PROMISE. CARRY ON.
JUST ONE THING!
KEEP MY ANKLES... TRIM, WOULD YOU?
LET'S KEEP OUR HOOVES AND HEARTS CROSSED, PARDNERS.

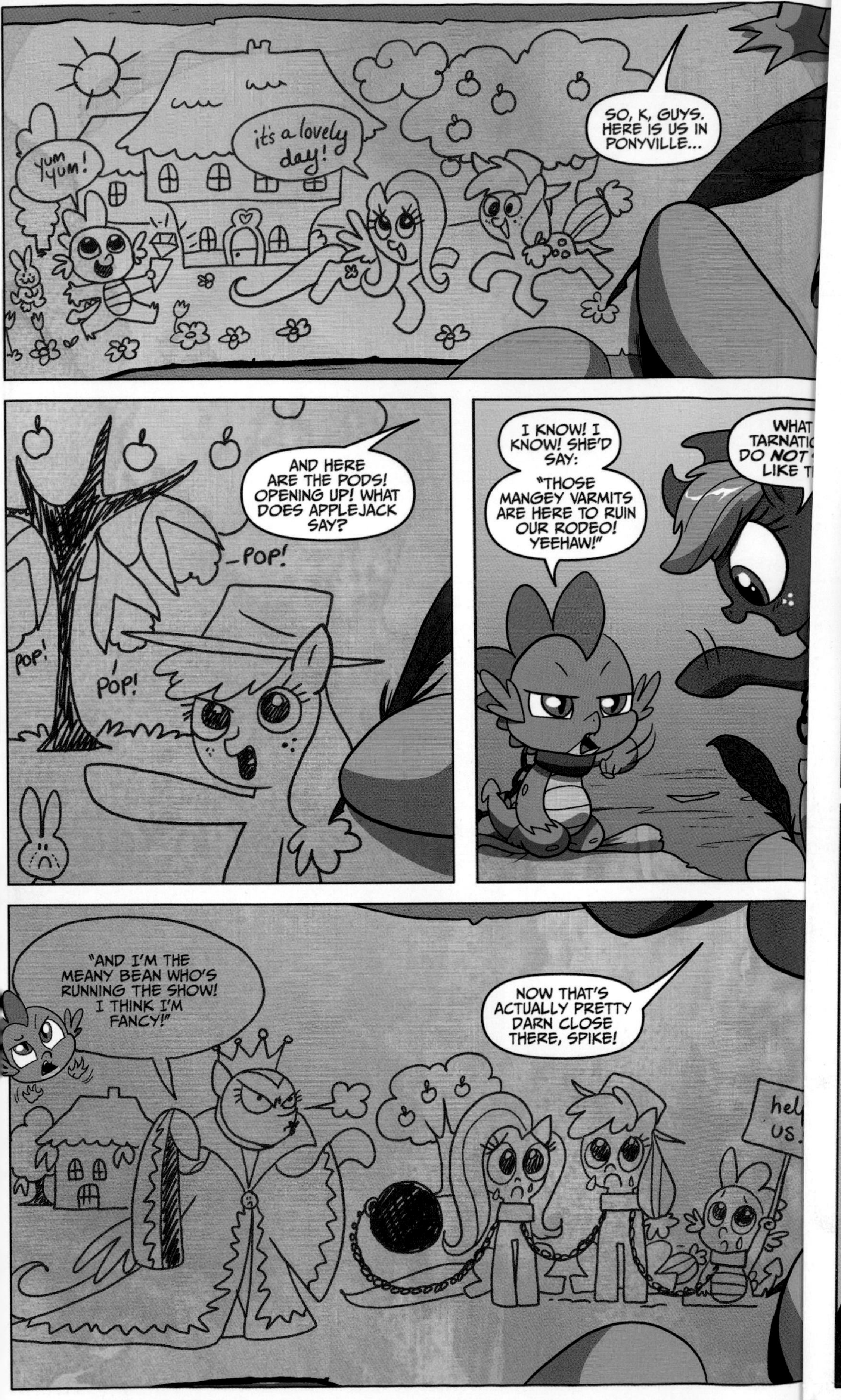

yum yum!
it's a lovely day!
SO, K, GUYS. HERE IS US IN PONYVILLE...
AND HERE ARE THE PODS! OPENING UP! WHAT DOES APPLEJACK SAY?
POP!
POP!
POP!
I KNOW! I KNOW! SHE'D SAY: "THOSE MANGEY VARMITS ARE HERE TO RUIN OUR RODEO! YEEHAW!"
WHAT TARNATIO DO NOT LIKE T
"AND I'M THE MEANY BEAN WHO'S RUNNING THE SHOW! I THINK I'M FANCY!"
NOW THAT'S ACTUALLY PRETTY DARN CLOSE THERE, SPIKE!
hel US

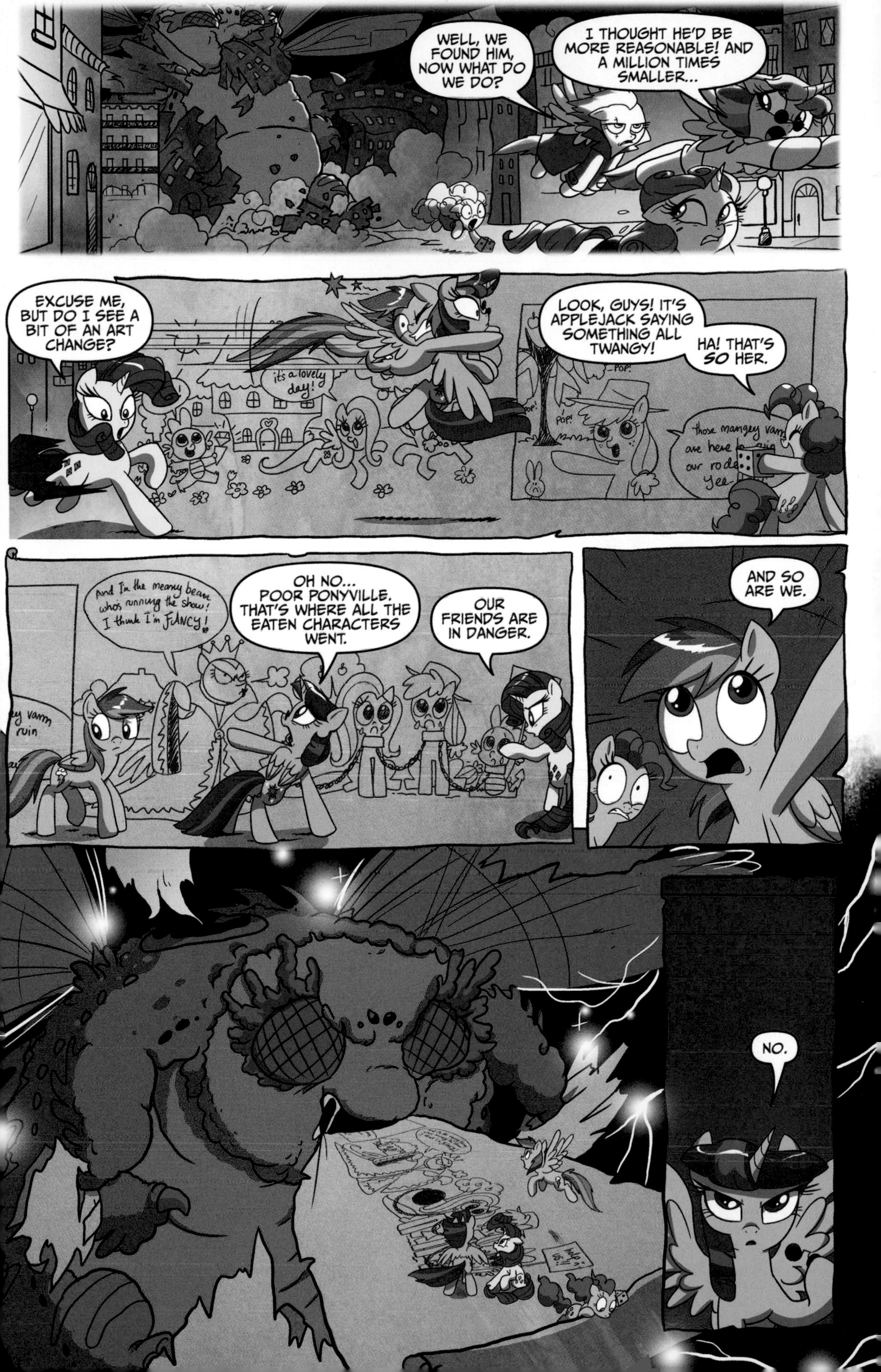
WELL, WE FOUND HIM, NOW WHAT DO WE DO?
I THOUGHT HE'D BE MORE REASONABLE! AND A MILLION TIMES SMALLER...
EXCUSE ME, BUT DO I SEE A BIT OF AN ART CHANGE?
it's a lovely day!
LOOK, GUYS! IT'S APPLEJACK SAYING SOMETHING ALL TWANGY!
HA! THAT'S SO HER.
those mangey vam
are here to ruin
our rode
Yee-
And I'm the meany beam who's running the show! I think I'm FANCY!
OH NO... POOR PONYVILLE. THAT'S WHERE ALL THE EATEN CHARACTERS WENT.
OUR FRIENDS ARE IN DANGER.
AND SO ARE WE.
NO.

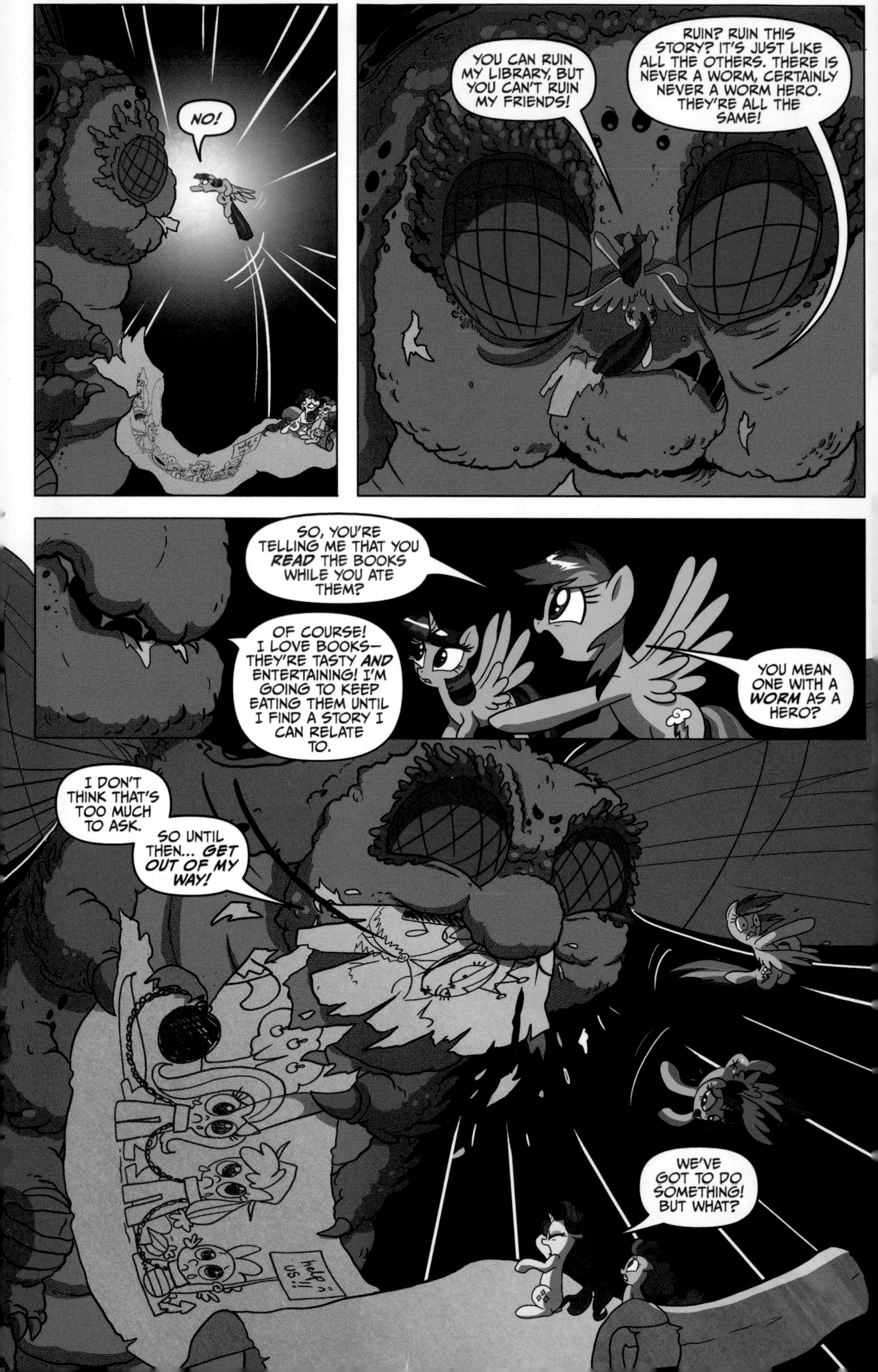
NO!
YOU CAN RUIN MY LIBRARY, BUT YOU CAN'T RUIN MY FRIENDS!
RUIN? RUIN THIS STORY? IT'S JUST LIKE ALL THE OTHERS. THERE IS NEVER A WORM, CERTAINLY NEVER A WORM HERO. THEY'RE ALL THE SAME!
SO, YOU'RE TELLING ME THAT YOU READ THE BOOKS WHILE YOU ATE THEM?
OF COURSE! I LOVE BOOKS—THEY'RE TASTY AND ENTERTAINING! I'M GOING TO KEEP EATING THEM UNTIL I FIND A STORY I CAN RELATE TO.
YOU MEAN ONE WITH A WORM AS A HERO?
I DON'T THINK THAT'S TOO MUCH TO ASK.
SO UNTIL THEN... GET OUT OF MY WAY!
WE'VE GOT TO DO SOMETHING! BUT WHAT?

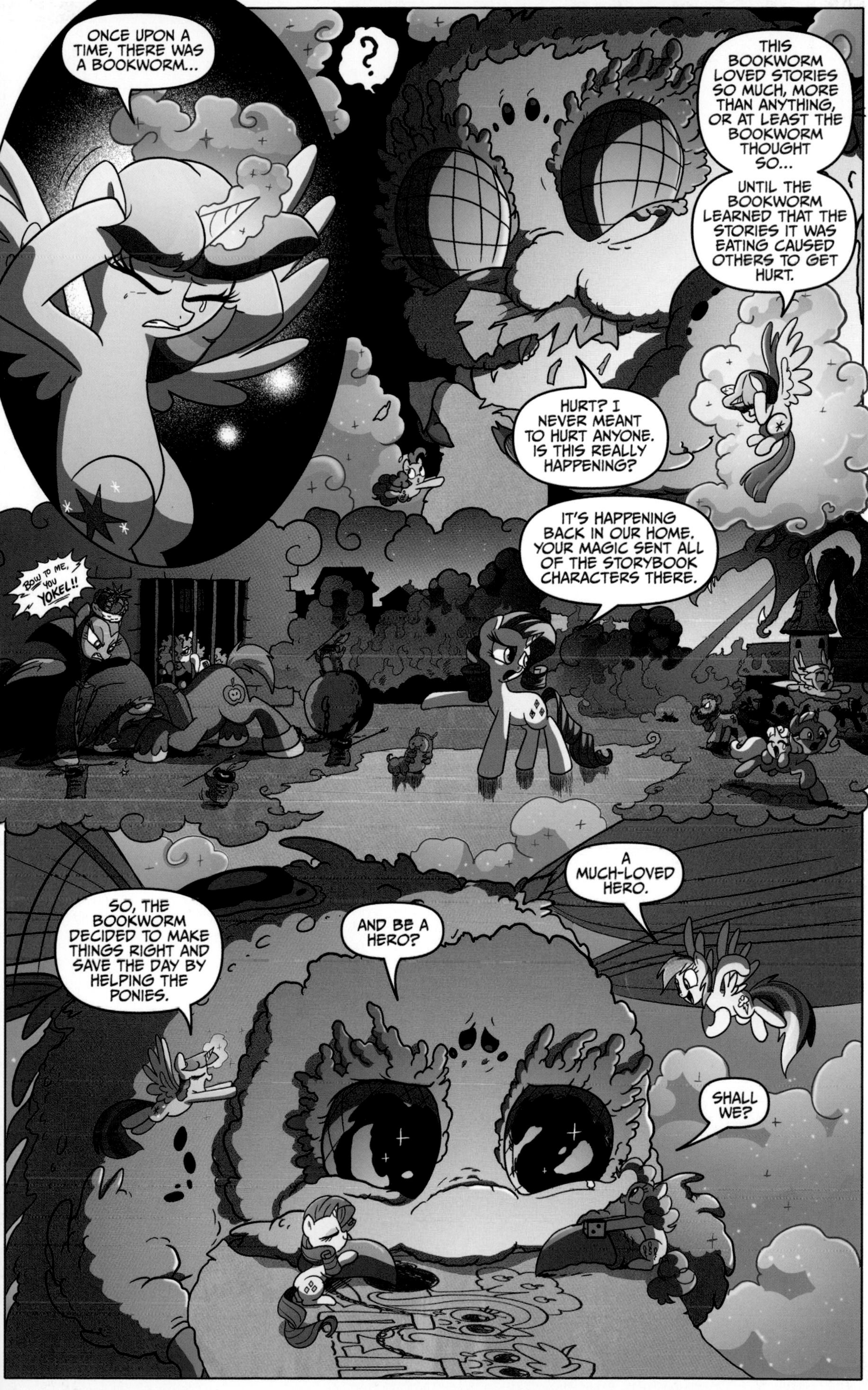
ONCE UPON A TIME, THERE WAS A BOOKWORM...
?
THIS BOOKWORM LOVED STORIES SO MUCH, MORE THAN ANYTHING, OR AT LEAST THE BOOKWORM THOUGHT SO...
UNTIL THE BOOKWORM LEARNED THAT THE STORIES IT WAS EATING CAUSED OTHERS TO GET HURT.
HURT? I NEVER MEANT TO HURT ANYONE. IS THIS REALLY HAPPENING?
IT'S HAPPENING BACK IN OUR HOME. YOUR MAGIC SENT ALL OF THE STORYBOOK CHARACTERS THERE.
BOW TO ME, YOU YOKEL!!
SO, THE BOOKWORM DECIDED TO MAKE THINGS RIGHT AND SAVE THE DAY BY HELPING THE PONIES.
AND BE A HERO?
A MUCH-LOVED HERO.
SHALL WE?

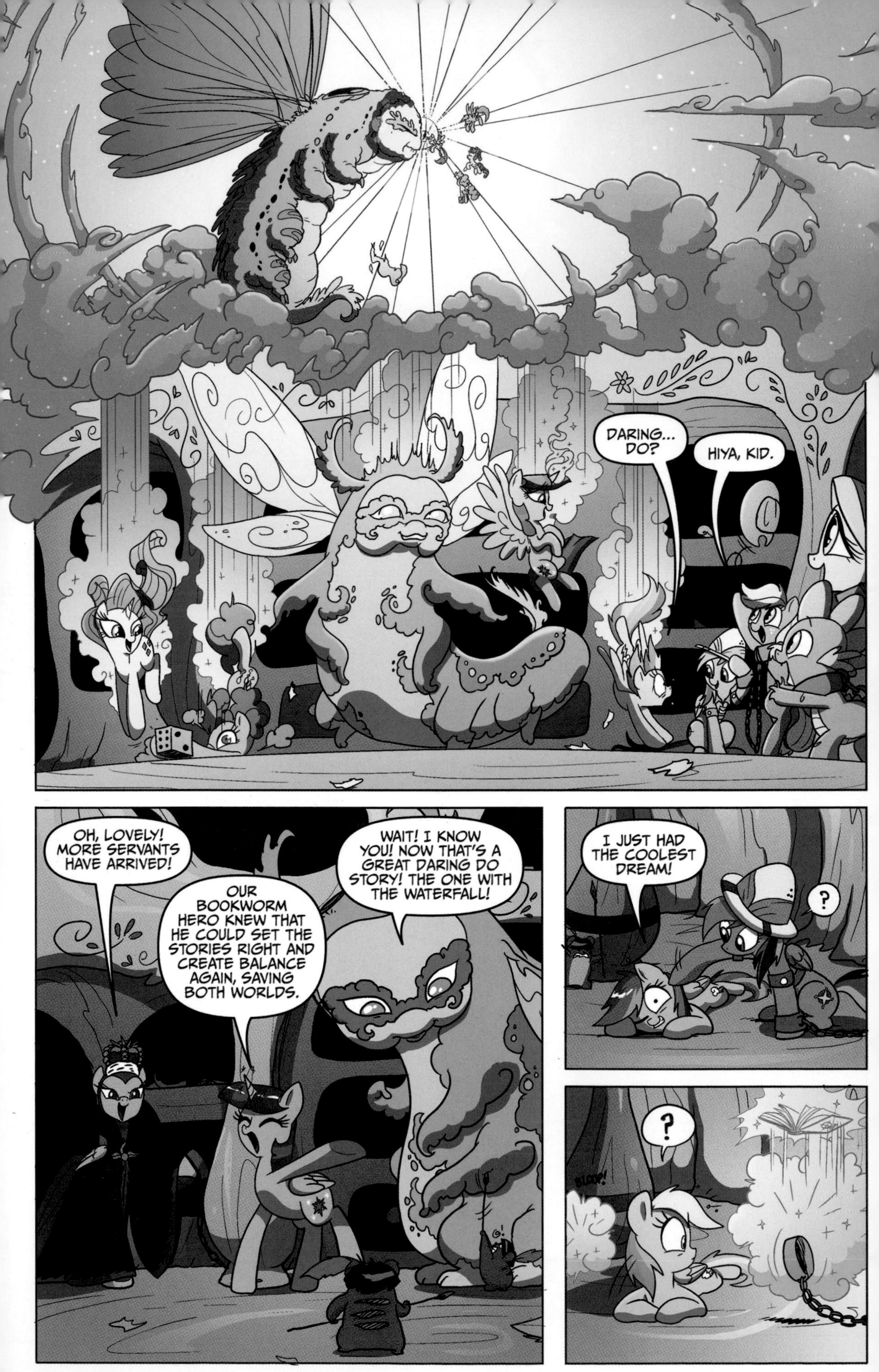
DARING... DO?
HIYA, KID.
OH, LOVELY! MORE SERVANTS HAVE ARRIVED!
OUR BOOKWORM HERO KNEW THAT HE COULD SET THE STORIES RIGHT AND CREATE BALANCE AGAIN, SAVING BOTH WORLDS.
WAIT! I KNOW YOU! NOW THAT'S A GREAT DARING DO STORY! THE ONE WITH THE WATERFALL!
I JUST HAD THE COOLEST DREAM!
?
?
BLOOP!

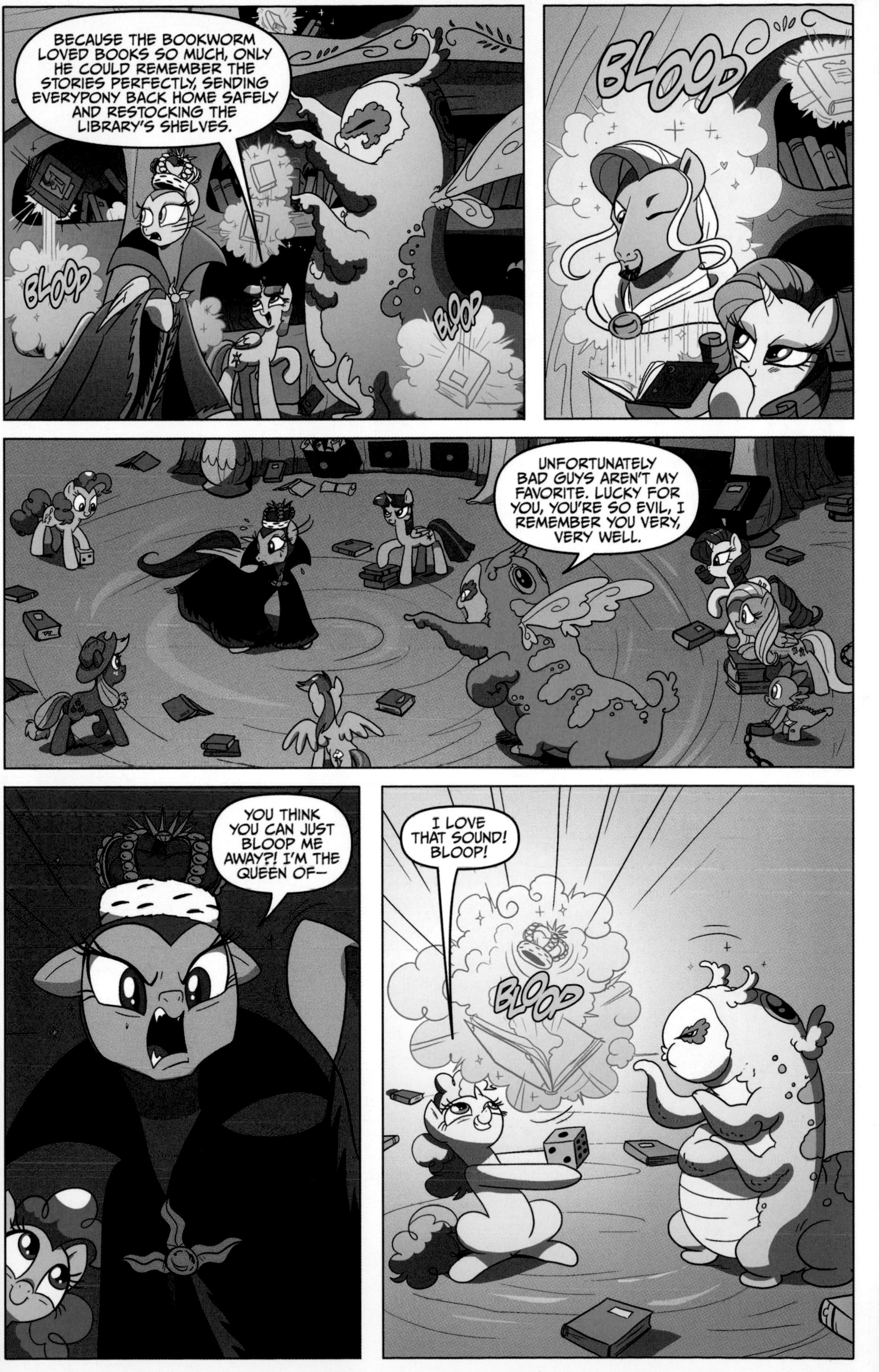
BECAUSE THE BOOKWORM LOVED BOOKS SO MUCH, ONLY HE COULD REMEMBER THE STORIES PERFECTLY, SENDING EVERYPONY BACK HOME SAFELY AND RESTOCKING THE LIBRARY'S SHELVES.
BLOOP
BLOOP
BLOOP
UNFORTUNATELY BAD GUYS AREN'T MY FAVORITE. LUCKY FOR YOU, YOU'RE SO EVIL, I REMEMBER YOU VERY, VERY WELL.
YOU THINK YOU CAN JUST BLOOP ME AWAY?! I'M THE QUEEN OF—
I LOVE THAT SOUND! BLOOP!
BLOOP

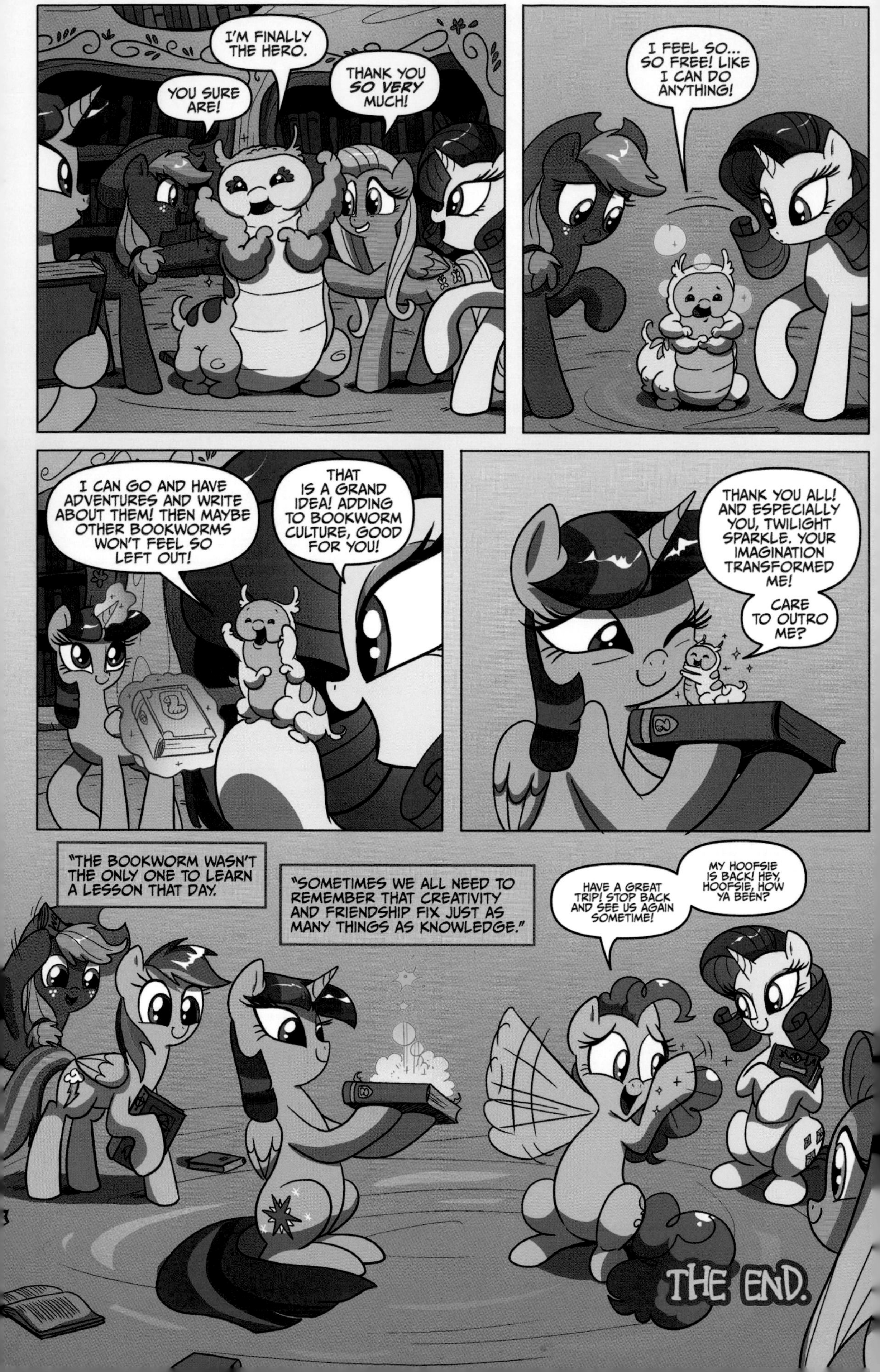
I'M FINALLY THE HERO.
YOU SURE ARE!
THANK YOU *SO VERY* MUCH!
I FEEL SO... SO FREE! LIKE I CAN DO ANYTHING!
I CAN GO AND HAVE ADVENTURES AND WRITE ABOUT THEM! THEN MAYBE OTHER BOOKWORMS WON'T FEEL SO LEFT OUT!
THAT IS A GRAND IDEA! ADDING TO BOOKWORM CULTURE, GOOD FOR YOU!
THANK YOU ALL! AND ESPECIALLY YOU, TWILIGHT SPARKLE. YOUR IMAGINATION TRANSFORMED ME!
CARE TO OUTRO ME?
"THE BOOKWORM WASN'T THE ONLY ONE TO LEARN A LESSON THAT DAY.
"SOMETIMES WE ALL NEED TO REMEMBER THAT CREATIVITY AND FRIENDSHIP FIX JUST AS MANY THINGS AS KNOWLEDGE."
HAVE A GREAT TRIP! STOP BACK AND SEE US AGAIN SOMETIME!
MY HOOFSIE IS BACK! HEY, HOOFSIE, HOW YA BEEN?
THE END.